You can be a Brownie Girl Scout, too!

If you are 6, 7, or 8 years old, or in the 1st, 2nd, or 3rd grade, just ask your parents to look in your local telephone directory under "Girl Scouts," and call for information. You can also ask your parents to call **Girl Scouts of the U.S.A.** at **1-(212) 852-8000** or write to 420 Fifth Avenue, New York, NY 10018-2702 to find out about becoming a Girl Scout in your area.

For everyone at Howell Living History Farm in
Titusville, New Jersey, and with special
thanks to Pete Watson and Susan DeVore
—M. L.

For Trisha
—L. S. L.

Copyright © 1996 by Girl Scouts of the United States of America. All rights reserved.
Published by Grosset & Dunlap, Inc., a member of The Putnam & Grosset Group, New
York, in cooperation with Girl Scouts of the United States of America. GROSSET &
DUNLAP is a trademark of Grosset & Dunlap, Inc. Published simultaneously in
Canada. Printed in the U.S.A.

Library of Congress Cataloging-in-Publication Data

Leonard, Marcia.
    Krissy and the big snow / by Marcia Leonard ; illustrated by
Laurie Struck Long.
        p.   cm. — (Here come the Brownies ; 12)
    "A Brownie Girl Scout book."
    Summary: When Krissy and her Brownie friends get snowed in on a visit to an
old-time working farm, they try to find ways to keep Krissy from feeling bad about
missing opening night in her first real play.
    [1. Girl Scouts—Fiction.   2. Plays—Fiction.   3. Farm life—Fiction.]
I. Long, Laurie Struck, ill.   II. Title.   III. Series.
PZ7.L549Kr   1996
[Fic]—dc20   95-36195
                                                                CIP
ISBN 0-448-40886-4   A B C D E F G H I J   AC

HERE COME THE BROWNIES
A Brownie Girl Scout Book

Krissy and the Big Snow

By Marcia Leonard
Illustrated by Laurie Struck Long

Grosset & Dunlap • New York
In association with GIRL SCOUTS OF THE U.S.A.

1

"I see it! I see the sleigh and the horses!" Krissy S. cried as the van pulled into the parking lot.

It was Saturday, and the Brownie Girl Scouts were on a special trip to a farm outside town. They were going to do all kinds of fun stuff, starting with an old-fashioned sleigh ride!

Krissy couldn't wait. She was the first to get out of the van. And the first to climb aboard the big old open sleigh.

The sleigh driver was a friendly looking man with bushy gray eyebrows. Krissy liked him right away.

"Welcome to Hawk Hill Farm!" he said. "I'm Hank Loudon—tour guide, farmer, and all-around good guy—at your service." He took off his old felt hat and wiggled his eyebrows up and down.

Krissy and the other Brownies giggled.

"Once we leave the parking lot, you can say good-bye to modern times," said Hank. "Hawk Hill Farm is a living history museum. That means we do things the way they were done a hundred years ago, so visitors can see what life was like back then." He grinned at the girls. "Are you ready for a trip to the past?"

"Ready!" they all shouted.

"Then hang on to your hats! Here we

go!" Hank called. He jammed his own hat back on his head. Then he snapped the reins over his farm horses' broad backs. "Get up, Salt. Get up, Pepper."

Krissy grabbed hold of the sideboard on the sleigh. There was a jerk. Then they were off, gliding down a snow-covered lane.

"Wheeee!" cried Jo Ann. "This is fun!"

"It sure is!" Krissy said happily. She loved the jingle-jingle of the sleigh bells and the feel of the frosty air on her face—especially since the rest of her was toasty warm beneath a big woolly sleigh blanket!

As the sleigh crossed a wooden bridge, Krissy started to sing: "Over the river and through the woods, to Hawk Hill Farm we go...."

The other Brownies joined in. So did their leader, Mrs. Quinones, and the moms who'd come along. Then the sleigh rounded a bend. "Whoa!" Hank said, and the horses stopped.

Up ahead, Krissy could see an L-shaped white house with black shutters. Nearby was a big red barn with smaller buildings around it.

"There it is—Hawk Hill Farm," said Hank. "Just imagine...one hundred years ago, half of you would have lived on a farm like this. And you would have done most of the work by hand—or with horses like Salt and Pepper."

"That sounds hard," said Lauren.

"It was!" said Hank. "And you wouldn't have had visitors come to help out with the chores, the way we do on this farm."

Krissy smiled. She was looking forward to the helping-out part. She and the other

Brownies were going to collect sap from the farm's maple trees to make into syrup.

"Get up!" Hank called to the horses, and the sleigh started gliding again.

"The farm looks so pretty—like a painting," Corrie said.

"It sure does," said Mrs. Q. "All we need now is a little falling snow to finish the picture."

Just then the sun disappeared behind the clouds...and a few fat snowflakes drifted down from the sky.

"Wow! Perfect timing, Mrs. Q.!" said Amy.

"Thank you, thank you." Mrs. Q. gave a little bow.

Krissy caught some snowflakes on her mitten. "Too bad they're all clumped together," she said. "You can't see the shapes."

"Yeah," said Amy, "but it makes them easier to catch." She tipped her head back and stuck out her tongue.

"I wish it would snow really, really hard," said Lauren. "It would be so cool if we got snowed in."

"Don't say that!" Krissy said quickly. "I have to be at the theater in time for *Beauty and the Beast*. It's our opening night!"

"Ooops! I forgot," said Lauren.

"Don't worry, Krissy," said Sarah's mom. "The weather report said light snow. Nothing more."

"That's good!" said Krissy.

"Are you nervous about tonight?" Sarah asked her. "I sure would be!"

"I'm more excited than nervous," said Krissy. "I can't believe I'm going to be in a real play with real actors. And at the Old Mill Theater, too! The exact same place we saw *The Secret Garden.*"

"Hey, guys! We know a big star," said Marsha.

Krissy laughed. "Wait a minute. I'm not a star yet. I only have one line. I say, 'Good morning, Belle.' Then I hand her a flower from my basket."

"Well, you're a star to *us,*" said Jo Ann.

"That's right!" said Mrs. Q. "The whole troop is excited about seeing you in the show next Saturday!"

"Thanks," said Krissy.

She stared at the gently falling snow. But she didn't really see it. Instead, she pictured herself in her costume—a long, pink dress with white silk roses at the waist.

She couldn't wait to step out on stage. To say her line. To perform for hundreds of people. Her sister, Maggie, her parents, and her grandparents would be there to watch her. And there was going to be a party for the actors afterward....

"*Good* morning, *Belle.* Good *morning,* Belle." Krissy practiced the words different ways in her head. Tonight at eight o'clock, the curtain would go up. And then she would say her line for real!

2

The sleigh stopped in front of the barn, and a woman pushed open the big wide doors.

"Hi, Ruth! Come and meet the Brownie Girl Scouts," called Hank. "Girls, this is my wife, Ruth. We run the farm together."

Ruth Loudon had snow-white hair tucked into a red stocking cap, and a smile that showed off her dimples. Krissy thought she looked like Mrs. Santa Claus.

"Welcome!" said Ruth. "Climb on

down, and I'll show you around. Then we'll start the maple sugaring."

Krissy and the others got down from the sleigh, while Hank unhitched Salt and Pepper.

"Wow! Those horses are humongous!" said Corrie. "They didn't seem so big when we were in the sleigh."

"Farm horses have to be big—and strong—because of all the hauling and plowing and other heavy work they do," said Ruth. "Salt and Pepper weigh around sixteen hundred pounds each. That's about six hundred pounds more than a riding horse weighs."

There were four more big horses in the barn. Krissy read the names on their stalls. " 'Thunder and Lightning,' 'Peanut Butter and Jelly.' " She giggled. "Who gave them those funny names?" she asked Hank.

"Don't blame me!" Hank held up both hands. "Kids name all the animals around here."

Next the troop met a cow named Mooreen and a bunch of clucking hens. Then they went on to the pig barn. In one pen, a big pig lay fast asleep. In another, four baby pigs were snuffling around in their trough, making a big mess.

"Hey, guys! Where are your manners?" joked Sarah. "You've got food on your noses!"

"And in your ears!" said Krissy. "You are even messier than my little brothers."

Thinking about Riley and Tyler made Krissy smile. The twins loved to hear her tell stories. And they were her best audience when she practiced her scene for the play.

"Good morning, Belle," she said softly. She held out her hand and made a little curtsy. Then she realized that Ruth was looking at her.

"The pig's name is Fifi," Ruth said, sounding puzzled, "not Belle."

Krissy's face felt hot. How embarrassing! She hadn't meant to say her line out loud! She cleared her throat. "Oh, right. Fifi. Cute name," she said, trying to sound casual.

I've got to stop thinking about the play!

she told herself. *At least while I'm here on the farm.*

The next stop was the sheep barn. After the brightness of the snow outside, the inside of the small barn seemed very dark. It was a moment before Krissy's eyes adjusted, and she saw that there were two young women working in the barn.

One was pitching fresh straw down from the hayloft. The other was spreading it around an empty pen. Both had on faded jeans and high rubber boots. They looked so much alike, Krissy was sure they were sisters.

"Girls, meet Rosa and Linda Navarro, two of our best farmhands," said Ruth. "They're both in college. But they help us out on weekends—and in the summer, too."

"Glad to meet you," said the sisters. They put down their pitchforks and joined the Brownie Girl Scouts at the sheep pen.

Krissy counted eight sheep.

"Boy, are they round!" said Marsha.

Rosa laughed. "Most of that is wool. Come back in the spring, when we shear them. Then you can see how skinny they are underneath."

"Some of them are also about to be mamas—like Gretel here," said Linda. She patted one of the roundest sheep.

"When is she going to have her baby?" asked Lauren.

"Maybe today," said Rosa. "That's why we're getting the new pen ready."

"Wow...a brand-new lamb!" Sarah's eyes were shining.

"I tell you what," said Ruth. "If you girls are still here when it's born, you can name it."

"Really? That would be great!" said Corrie.

"Yeah," said Marsha. "But there are so many names to choose from. How will we ever pick one?"

"Easy," said Amy. "Just start at the beginning of the alphabet—with A for Amy."

The other girls laughed.

"It might be a boy, you know," said Sarah.

"Let's wait and see," said Mrs. Q. "*Then* you can think of a name. Okay?"

"Okay," said the Brownies.

But Krissy was sure she knew the perfect names already. Belle for a girl, and Prince for a boy—just like in *Beauty and the Beast*.

3

Ruth steadied the tip of a drill against the side of the maple tree. "Okay, Corrie, turn the handle," she said. "When the hole we're making is two inches deep, we'll put in the wooden tap. Then we'll hook on the bucket to catch the sap."

Corrie started turning. "Are you sure this won't hurt the tree?" she asked anxiously.

"Positive," said Ruth. "In three weeks or so, we'll take out the tap. Then the hole will close by itself."

"But doesn't the tree need the sap?" asked Krissy.

"We take only a little of what the tree makes," said Ruth. "Believe me, there will be plenty left over to help the new leaves grow in spring."

Corrie finished drilling the hole. Then Sarah put in the tap, and Krissy hooked on the bucket. When the first drop of sap appeared, Ruth said, "You can taste it, if you like."

Krissy caught the drop on her finger and licked it up. "Hey! It's not like maple syrup at all!" she said. "It's watery and hardly even sweet."

"It will be, once we boil it down," said Ruth. "Wait till we get to the sugar house. You'll see."

The girls took the full buckets of sap from the other trees. They emptied them into two tall containers set on a flat wooden sleigh. Then Thunder and Lightning hauled the sleigh to the sugar house.

As Krissy walked along behind them, she noticed that the wind had picked up. It sent the snowflakes swirling. And it piled up little drifts on the path.

Good thing I wore big boots! she thought.

The sugar house had a low roof and no windows. Ruth pointed to a long, wide pan set on a brick furnace. "That's the evaporator," she said. "It boils the water out of the sap. What's left is syrup."

Krissy sniffed the golden-brown liquid. "Mmmm! Smells good!"

"This batch is done," said Hank. "I don't suppose any of you would like a taste...."

"Yes! Yes!" cried all the girls.

Ruth poured some of the syrup through a filter. "This will catch any bits of bark or leaves that fell into the sap bucket," she explained.

Then Hank poured the filtered syrup into tiny paper cups and handed them around.

"Delicious!" said Mrs. Q.

"Uh-huh!" said Lauren. "It sure would be great with some pancakes."

Hank patted his pockets. "Sorry. I thought I had a couple on me. But I'm fresh out," he said. Then he wiggled his eyebrows.

Krissy and the other Brownie Girl Scouts giggled.

"Don't worry," said Ruth. "When we're done here, we'll give you some syrup to take home. You can have it for breakfast tomorrow."

The girls put the rest of the syrup through the filter. They poured it into rows of sparkling glass jars and fastened the lids on tight. Then they glued on pretty labels. By the time they had finished, most of the afternoon was gone.

Hank filled the evaporator with the sap the Brownies had collected. "We're all done for now," he said. "You've been a big help, girls."

Ruth gave them each a little jar of syrup to take home. "If you have time, I'd like to show you the farmhouse," she said. "The part Hank and I live in is pretty modern. But the old part looks the way a farmhouse did a hundred years ago. So you can see what life was like without electricity and running water."

"That sounds neat," said Krissy. "Can we, Mrs. Q.?"

"And can we go see Gretel again, too?" asked Sarah. "Maybe she's had her baby by now."

Mrs. Q. checked her watch. "I think we have time for both," she said.

"Great," said Hank. "I'll go hitch up the sleigh for the ride back to the parking lot."

He opened the door, and the Brownies stepped outside—right into the middle of a blizzard!

4

The Brownies stood in the doorway of the sugar house and stared out at the storm. Krissy could not believe her eyes. The snow was coming down so thick and fast, she could hardly see the white farmhouse!

"What happened!?" she cried. "This isn't light snow!"

"It sure isn't!" said Sarah's mom. "I hope the snowplows are out. Or we may have trouble getting back to town."

Krissy's stomach turned over. "Please, Mrs. Q., can we leave right now?" she begged. "I have to go home and get ready for the play."

Mrs. Q. gave her a quick hug. "I know," she said kindly. "But it wouldn't be safe to drive in this weather. We'll have to wait till the storm passes over and we can see where we're going."

"How long will that be?" wailed Krissy.

"Not long—I hope!" said Mrs. Q.

"Let's go up to the farmhouse," Ruth said. "We can listen to the weather report on the radio. Then you'll know better what to do."

The girls joined hands and followed the Loudons to the farmhouse. But it was slow going. The heavy snow blinded them. The deep drifts pulled at their boots. And the wind blew so hard it almost knocked them over.

As Krissy fought her way toward the house, she tried not to worry. After all, it was still hours before show time. The storm couldn't last *much* longer.

Or could it?

The farmhouse was cold and dark when they finally arrived. Krissy tried to find a light switch. Then she remembered. There was no electricity in this part of the house.

Hank lit some kerosene lamps, and Ruth built cheerful fires in the two fireplaces—one in the dining room, and one in the parlor. Soon the rooms were nice and cozy.

Krissy looked around at the old-fashioned furniture. In the glowing lamplight, she could almost imagine she'd gone back in time. But right now, she was more interested in something up-to-date—the weather report on the Loudon's portable radio.

She perched on one of the stiff parlor chairs and listened hard.

"A surprise snowstorm hit town today,"

said the reporter. "Skies will clear later this evening, but drifting snow has already closed most country roads. Police ask drivers in those areas to stay home until tomorrow...."

Hank turned down the radio. "Well, there you have it, girls. You're snowed in!"

Krissy froze. *Snowed in!* The words seemed to echo in her ears. Then all around her, the Brownies started talking.

"Yippee!"

"Wow! I can't believe it!"

"Can we really stay here, Mrs. Q.?"

"Where will we sleep?"

Jo Ann took Krissy's hand. "What about Krissy's play?" she said loudly. "She's going to miss opening night!"

"Oh, no! That's right!" said Marsha. She and the other girls gathered around Krissy.

"I'm really sorry," said Corrie.

"You'll still be in it tomorrow night," said Amy.

"And next Saturday, too, when we come to see you," said Sarah.

Krissy knew her friends were trying to make her feel better. But they didn't understand. "It's not the same!" she cried. "Opening night is special. It happens only once." Then she burst into tears.

Mrs. Q. knelt beside her. "You're right. Opening night *is* special. And I'm so sorry you're going to miss it, Krissy. But there's just no safe way to get you to the theater."

"I know," Krissy said through her tears. Ruth handed her a clean hankie. It was soft and smelled like roses. Slowly, Krissy's sobs turned to sniffles.

"Are you okay?" asked Mrs. Q.

Krissy nodded. Her tears were all gone. Now she just felt numb.

Mrs. Q. turned to the Loudons. "I never thought our visit would turn into a sleepover!" she said. "I hope it's not a problem."

"Not to worry," said Hank. "We can have pancakes with maple syrup for supper. And you all can bed down on the parlor floor—snug as a bug in a rug." He wiggled his eyebrows and grinned.

"Honestly, it will be fun!" said Ruth.

"Thanks!" said Mrs. Q. She looked around the old-fashioned room. "Is there any way we can call the girls' families?"

"Sure," said Ruth. "There's a phone upstairs, where Hank and I live."

"Krissy," Mrs. Q. said, "why don't you call first?"

While the rest of the troop headed for the

kitchen, Mrs. Q. took Krissy to the phone.
First she told Krissy's mother what had
happened. Then she handed the receiver
to Krissy.

"Mom?" Krissy's voice wavered.

"Oh, sweetie! I'm so sorry," said her
mom. "I know you were looking forward
to tonight. We all were! But you're safe and
sound. That's what really matters."

Krissy swallowed hard. "Will you call the
theater and tell them why I can't make it?"

"Of course," said her mother. "And
Krissy, as far as we are concerned, the play
doesn't open until *you* are in it. So we'll
have our own opening-night party when you
get back."

"Thanks, Mom. I love you," said Krissy.
She felt as if her mother had given her a big,
warm hug.

5

Krissy peeked into the kitchen. The other Brownies were talking and laughing and having a good time. None of them seemed to mind being snowed in!

Ruth waved and came over. "Hi," she said. "We're making pancakes the old-fashioned way. Come and see." She took Krissy's hand and led her into the room.

One group of girls was helping Hank build a wood fire in the big iron stove.

Another group was using an old-time churn to turn milk into butter.

Corrie, Amy, Marsha, and Sarah were over at the kitchen counter. "Look at this, Krissy! Isn't it neat?" Amy pointed to an odd-looking metal machine.

"What is it?" asked Krissy.

"A wheat grinder," said Corrie. "See? You put the wheat in here, at the top. Then you turn the handle to grind it up. And flour comes out the bottom."

The flour was speckled, like the whole-wheat flour Krissy's father used when he baked bread.

"Do you want to try it?" asked Marsha.

"I guess so," said Krissy.

"Good," said Ruth. "Then I'll go get us some eggs from the henhouse." She put on her coat and stocking cap and headed out the door.

Krissy turned the handle of the wheat grinder. But her thoughts were miles away, on a stage at the Old Mill Theater. And she didn't mind when it was time for Amy to take her place.

She wandered into the parlor and gazed out the window at the snow. Then someone tapped her shoulder.

"Krissy? I have to talk to you." It was Lauren, and she looked upset.

"What's the matter?" Krissy asked.

Lauren took a deep breath. "I just want to say that I wish I'd never made that wish!" she said in a rush.

Krissy looked at her blankly. "What wish?"

"You know! About getting snowed in!" said Lauren. "It was a dumb thing to say, and now you're missing your play and everything...."

"Oh, Lauren! That's silly," said Krissy. "You didn't *make* the snow fall by wishing."

"Maybe not. But I feel bad anyway," said Lauren. "I wish I could find a way to cheer you up."

"I'm okay. Really," said Krissy. She didn't want to be cheered up. What she wanted was to crawl in bed and pull the covers over her head until morning. But it was hours before lights-out.

It was going to be a long night.

*   *   *

"Seconds, anyone?" Sarah carried a big platter of pancakes in from the kitchen.

"Me, please!" said Krissy. She hadn't felt much like eating at first. But everything was so yummy—especially the maple syrup. It was much better than the kind from the store.

As she helped herself from the platter, Linda and Rosa came in. Their cheeks were pink from the cold. And little white snowflakes clung to their dark hair.

"It's still snowing, I see," said Mrs. Q.

"Yes, but not as hard as before," said Linda. "And the wind has stopped all together—thank goodness!"

The sisters pulled two straight-backed chairs up to the long dining table.

"Has Gretel had her baby yet?" Sarah asked.

"Not yet," said Rosa. She smiled at Sarah. "I can still remember the first time *I* saw a brand-new lamb. So we'll let you know when this one is born. Promise."

After dinner, the Brownie Girl Scouts cleared the table. Since there was no running water in the house, they went outside to pump water from the well. Then they heated the water on the wood stove and did the dishes.

"That was fun!" Jo Ann's mom said when the last plate was dried. "But imagine hauling wood and water every time you washed dishes or took a bath."

"Really," said Sarah's mom. "Now I know why old-time farmers went to bed so early. They were completely worn out!"

"Mom! You're not really tired, are you?" said Sarah. "It's only seven o'clock."

One hour till curtain time, thought Krissy. *I should be at the theater right now. Getting made up. Putting on my beautiful dress. And then . . .* She sighed deeply.

Jo Ann looked over at her. "Are you thinking about the play?" she asked.

Krissy nodded sadly.

Suddenly, Lauren's eyes opened wide. "Hey! I know! Let's put on a play here," she said. "It wouldn't be *Beauty and the Beast*, but it might make you feel better, Krissy."

"What a good idea!" said Ruth.

"What do you say, Krissy?" said Corrie.

"Please?" begged the other girls.

Krissy frowned. Putting on a play was about the last thing she wanted to do. It would only remind her of all she was missing! But her friends looked so excited, she couldn't say no.

"All right," she said, forcing herself to smile. "If *you* really want to."

"Great! What play should we do?" said Amy. "I vote for something funny."

"How about something with dancing?" said Marsha.

"Anything's fine with me," said Sarah,

"as long as I don't have a lot of lines!"

Other girls chimed in.

At first Krissy just listened. But finally she couldn't help jumping in too. "Guys? Guys! We're not getting anywhere. We need a director," she said.

Lauren grinned. "Okay, Krissy, you just got yourself a job!"

6

"I didn't mean *I* should be the director!" said Krissy. But everyone was looking at her and waiting for her to tell them what to do. "Well," she said slowly, "I could teach you an acting game I learned in my theater class."

"Go for it, Krissy," said Amy.

So Krissy did. First she divided the girls into teams. Then she asked Rosa and Linda to write a bunch of funny words on slips of paper. "Like armadillo ... banana ... Frisbee.

The sillier the better," she said.

When they were done,
Krissy put the slips
into a hat. "Okay,"
she said. "Each team
makes up a little
play using three special
words. Everyone gets the same first word—"

"How about 'farm'?" called out Hank.

"Great!" said Krissy. "Then each team
picks two more words from the hat. We
have half an hour to think up our plays.
And after that, it's show time!"

"Cool!" said Amy. "Can I pick the words
for my team?" She reached into the hat and
took out two slips. " 'Noodles' and 'tuba.'
Boy, this isn't going to be easy!"

Lauren, Corrie, Sarah, and Jo Ann were

on Krissy's team. Corrie picked out their words—"dragon" and "popcorn." Then they went into a huddle.

"Okay," Krissy said a little later. "Let's go over what we've got so far."

Corrie started. "There's this mean dragon who lives in the mountains—that's me. And she likes to fly down to the farm and make trouble. She burns the crops with her fire-breath. And she scares the animals—"

"I'll act out the animals," put in Sarah. "That way I won't have to say a thing!"

"I'll be a farmhand," said Jo Ann. "You can call me...um...Rosalinda."

"Perfect!" said Krissy. "Then Lauren can be Ruth. And I'll be Hank." She wiggled her eyebrows and grinned. "Welcome to Hawk Hill Farm," she said, exactly like Hank.

Her friends laughed.

"What an actress," said Lauren. "You should be on stage, Krissy."

Krissy's face fell. For a moment she'd forgotten about the play. The *real* play! But Lauren's words brought it all back. "You're right," she sighed. "I *should* be on stage. Right now—at the Old Mill Theater!"

Lauren blushed. "Me and my big mouth! Sorry, Krissy. I only meant..."

"I know, Lauren," said Krissy. "Let's just keep going. We don't have much time."

"And we still have to figure out how to get in the word 'popcorn,'" said Sarah.

"Not to worry!" Krissy said in her Hank voice. "I have an idea that just might work." And as her team huddled around her, she told them all about it.

Before Krissy knew it, it was show time!

Krissy's team went first. Corrie was a great dragon, gliding around the parlor. Krissy, Lauren, and Jo Ann were funny as the farmers. And Sarah acted out a whole barnful of animals. Then it was time for the last scene.

"Come on! Let's hide in the cornfield and wait for the dragon," said Lauren.

"Okay," said Jo Ann. "I just hope our plan works." She and Lauren and Krissy ducked out of sight behind the sofa. Sarah crawled after them, pretending to be a watchdog.

"Hold on to your hats!" Krissy cried in her Hank voice. "Here comes the dragon."

While Corrie swooped around a few times, the other girls got ready for their big ending. Krissy blew up a brown paper bag like a balloon and squeezed it shut. Sarah,

Lauren, and Jo Ann picked up crumpled bits of white paper they'd made before the show.

"Whooooosh!" breathed Corrie.

"Hooray! The dragon is heating up the corn," cried Lauren.

That was Krissy's cue. She hit the bottom of the bag hard. It made a loud *POP!* And at the same moment, the girls threw their paper bits high in the air.

"Popcorn!" they all shouted.

Corrie the dragon screeched loudly and raced away. The audience laughed. And the four girls came out from behind the sofa.

"That dragon will never bother us again," said Jo Ann.

"Good job!" said Lauren.

"Good popcorn," said Krissy. She picked up a handful of the paper popcorn and held it out to the audience. "I don't suppose any of you would like a taste," she said. And she wiggled her eyebrows like Hank.

Everyone clapped and cheered—Hank the loudest of all. The girls took a bow. Then they went and sat down in the audience.

Krissy was grinning from ear to ear. Maybe their play wasn't *Beauty and the Beast*, but she was proud of it—and putting it on sure had been fun.

She leaned over and gave Lauren's hand a squeeze. "Thanks," she said.

"What for?" asked Lauren.

"Your plan worked," said Krissy. "I feel a whole lot better."

"Great!" said Lauren. Then she giggled. "Hey! Another one of my wishes came true."

Krissy plopped down on the floor to watch the other teams. It was neat to see how they managed to use their three words. And the plays were so funny, she laughed till her tummy hurt.

All too soon, it was time to get ready for bed. Hank and Ruth went out to do their last chores. And Linda and Rosa went to check on Gretel. When they came back, all four of them were carrying sleigh blankets.

"You can use these for bedding," said Ruth. "It's going to be a cold night. But here's some good news. It finally stopped snowing!"

Krissy found a space near Sarah and her mom. She spread out her blanket on the floor. Then she rolled up her sweater to use as a pillow.

"Good night! Sweet dreams," said Ruth.

"Good night," said Hank. "And if you hear a bear growling, don't worry. It's just me snoring."

The Brownie Girl Scouts settled down. Slowly the room got quiet. But Krissy didn't go to sleep right away.

She thought about the play—and realized with a start that it was long over! Everyone would be at the party now. She tried to picture herself there with the other actors. Instead, she kept remembering all the fun things she'd done with her friends.

How weird! thought Krissy. *I'm sad and glad at the same time! Sad about missing opening night. But glad I got snowed in on the farm.*

It was all very confusing. And Krissy was suddenly too tired to think about it. She yawned and rolled over. The next moment, she was asleep.

7

Krissy woke up early the next morning. She stretched, yawned, and noticed that Sarah and her mom were already up.

"Good morning, early bird," whispered Sarah.

"Hi," Krissy whispered back. "You're up early, too."

"I guess I'm just in the habit," said Sarah. "My puppy, Muffin, never lets me sleep late at home. She licks my face to get me up."

Suddenly the front door opened. A blast of cold air swept into the parlor, waking Marsha and Lauren.

"Brrrr!" said Lauren. "Who let in the cold?" She snuggled deeper into her blanket.

Rosa peeked into the room. "Sorry. That was me," she whispered. "I just came to see if anyone was awake. Guess what? Gretel had her baby last night!"

Instantly, the four girls were on their feet. They jammed on their boots and grabbed their coats and hats and mittens.

Sarah's mom laughed softly. "Hey, wait for me! I want to see the lambs, too."

They left the rest of the Brownie Girl Scouts sleeping peacefully and hurried out into the crisp, cold air.

The snow sparkled in the early morning sun. And all the buildings looked as if they'd been frosted with vanilla icing. It was so pretty, Krissy stopped for just a moment to look. Then she raced to catch up with Rosa and the others.

Linda was waiting for them in Gretel's pen. And there, nestled in the sweet-smelling hay, was Gretel's baby. It had a chocolate-brown face and legs. And its grayish-brown wool was in tight little curls.

"Oh, it's so cute!" exclaimed Sarah.

"Is it a boy or a girl?" asked Marsha.

"A girl," said Linda. "Would you like to meet her? You can come in one by one."

Sarah went first. Then Lauren. Then it was Krissy's turn. She gently stroked the new lamb's head and back. She couldn't believe how soft she was. And how perfect.

"Let's go get everyone else," said Sarah. "They'll want to see the lamb, too." A few minutes later, the whole troop was in the barn.

Linda held up the lamb for everyone to see.

"Ooooooh!" said all the girls.

"So, what are you going to name her?" asked Rosa. "Remember, it's up to you."

"How about Stormy?" said Amy.

"Or maybe Snowflake?" said Corrie.

"I don't know," said Marsha. "Stormy sounds kind of rough for such a sweet baby. And she isn't white like snow." She turned to Krissy. "What do you think?"

"Well…" said Krissy, "I'd like to call her Belle."

"You mean like Belle in *Beauty and the Beast?*" asked Jo Ann.

"That's what I thought yesterday—when Ruth told us we could name the lamb," said Krissy. "But now I want to call her Belle because it means beautiful. And she's about the most beautiful thing I've ever seen!"

"Belle," said Mrs. Q., trying it out.

"I like it," said Sarah.

"Me too," said Lauren.

"And what do *you* think?" Krissy asked the lamb. "Do you like the name Belle?"

"Meeeh!" said the lamb.

"That's a definite yes," said Rosa. "Belle it is."

Everyone laughed.

Gretel was getting restless, pacing back

and forth in the pen. And Linda said it was time to leave mama and baby alone. As the girls trooped out of the barn, Krissy turned around for one last look at the lamb.

"Good morning, Belle," she called. Then she grinned. She finally got to say her line!

On the way back to the farmhouse, Amy scooped up a handful of snow. "All right! It's perfect for packing," she said. "Who wants to make a snowman?"

"I do! I do!" said the other Brownies.

"Not me. I'm going to make a snow *girl*," said Lauren. "Want to help, Krissy?"

"Sure," said Krissy.

They rolled three round balls and stacked them up. They added two sticks for arms. Then they got a carrot from Ruth to use for a nose. And buttons to use for twinkling eyes.

Krissy gave the snow girl one last pat. "There," she said. "I think she's finished."

"Not quite," said Lauren. "Something's missing—and I know just what it is! Stay here. I'll be right back."

She disappeared into the house for a moment. When she returned, she was carrying her Brownie sash and beanie. She put them on the snow girl.

"Ta-dah! It's a snow Brownie!" she said.

Krissy laughed. Then she flung her arms out wide. "This is so great!" she said.

"You mean our snow Brownie?" asked Lauren.

"I mean everything," said Krissy. "All the neat things we did yesterday. Our play. The sleep over. Belle. Everything!"

"Then you're not sorry that you missed opening night?" asked Lauren.

"Sure I am," said Krissy. "But I wouldn't have missed this for the world!"

Mrs. Q. stuck her head out the door. "Girls!" she called. "I just heard the news on the radio. The roads have been cleared. So we'll be leaving soon."

"Oh! Do we have to?" said Amy.

"We're having so much fun!" said Corrie.

Mrs. Q. laughed. "I know. It's been a wonderful adventure. But now it's time to head on home."

The Brownies brushed the snow off their clothes and went inside. The radio was still on in the parlor.

"Last night's heavy snowfall closed more than just the roads," the announcer was saying. "Here's a list of events that were canceled: Westwood High School's winter concert...the opening-night performance of *Beauty and the Beast* at the Old Mill Theater..."

Krissy didn't hear the rest of the list. She and the other Brownies were on their feet, cheering and laughing and dancing around the room.

The grown-ups all came rushing in.

"What is it?" asked Mrs. Q. "What are we celebrating?"

"Is it somebody's birthday?" asked Hank.

"Better than that!" said Krissy. "While we were snowed *in, Beauty and the Beast* was snowed *out*! I didn't miss opening night after all!"

Girl Scout Ways

Krissy and her troop had lots of fun learning the old-fashioned way to make things like flour, maple syrup, and butter. Even if you don't have an old-time butter churn, you and your friends can still make homemade butter all by yourselves!

- Here's what you'll need: a clean, empty baby food jar and some cold heavy cream.

- Fill the jar almost to the top with heavy cream and screw the lid on very, very tight.

- Now shake the jar—up and down...side to side... any way you like. (When your arm gets tired, let a friend take a turn.)

- Shake for about five minutes, then open the jar. Look—real homemade butter! (If it isn't butter yet, don't worry. Just screw the lid back on and shake some more.)

- You can also make homemade butter by whipping heavy cream up with an electric mixer, blender, or egg-beater. First, of course, you'll get whipped cream. But don't stop there. Butter comes next!